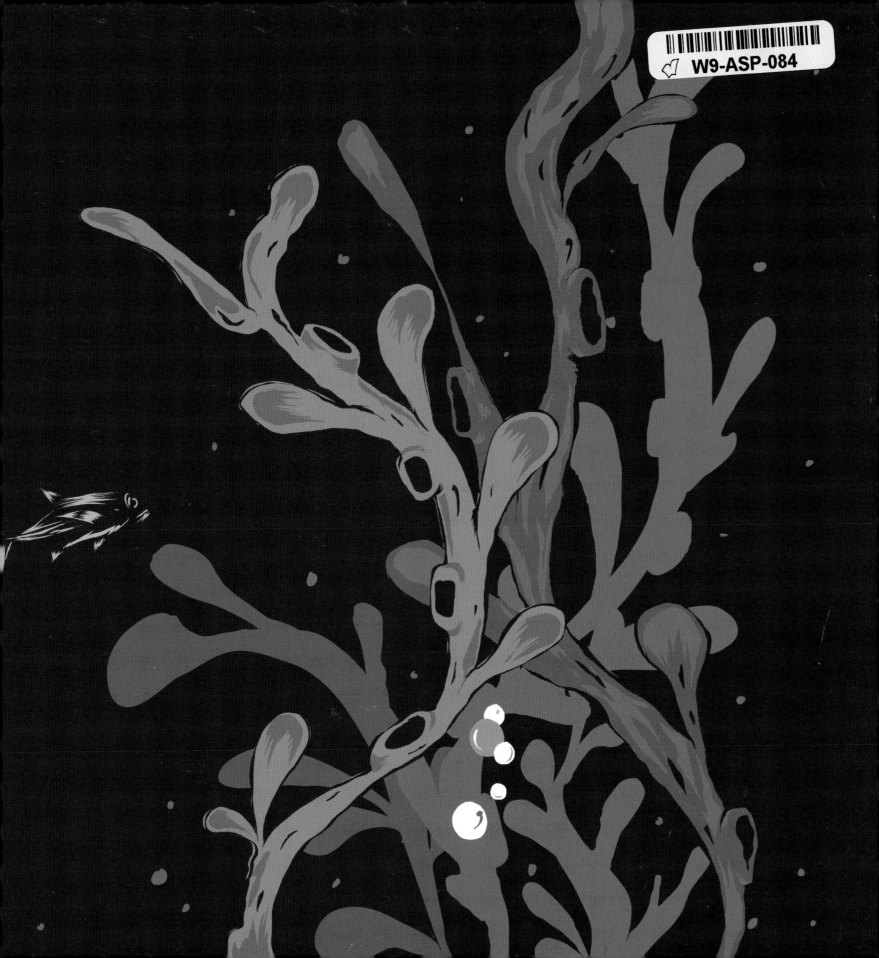

For my parents.
Thank you for guiding the way.

Copyright © 2015 by Ben Joel Price

All rights reserved. Published in the United States by Random House Children's Books,
a division of Random House LLC, a Penguin Random House Company, New York.

Random House and the colophon are registered trademarks of Random House LLC.

Visit us on the Web! randomhousekids.com

Educators and librarians, for a variety of teaching tools, visit us at RHTeachersLibrarians.com

Library of Congress Cataloging-in-Publication Data
Price, Ben Joel, author, illustrator.
In the deep dark deep / by Ben Joel Price. — First edition.
pages cm.
Summary: Deep Sea Diver, Robot, and Monkey board a submarine, the *Guppy,* to delve into the
darkest depths to discover what has taken the light from the sea.
ISBN 978-0-385-37313-5 (trade) — ISBN 978-0-375-97202-7 (lib. bdg.) — ISBN 978-0-375-98195-1 (ebook)
[1. Stories in rhyme. 2. Underwater exploration—Fiction. 3. Submarines (Ships)—Fiction. 4. Divers—Fiction.
5. Robots—Fiction. 6. Monkeys—Fiction.] I. Title.
PZ8.3.P916 In 2015 [E]—dc23 2014023133

MANUFACTURED IN CHINA

10 9 8 7 6 5 4 3 2 1

First Edition

IN THE DEEP DARK DEEP

Ben Joel Price

Random House 🏠 New York

Beneath a secret lighthouse
the light drained from the sea.
Down to the darkest depths we dive
to solve this mystery.

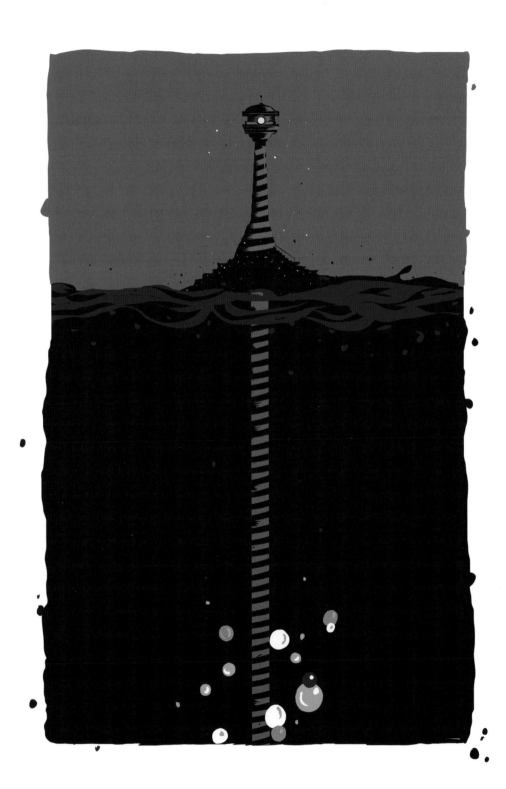

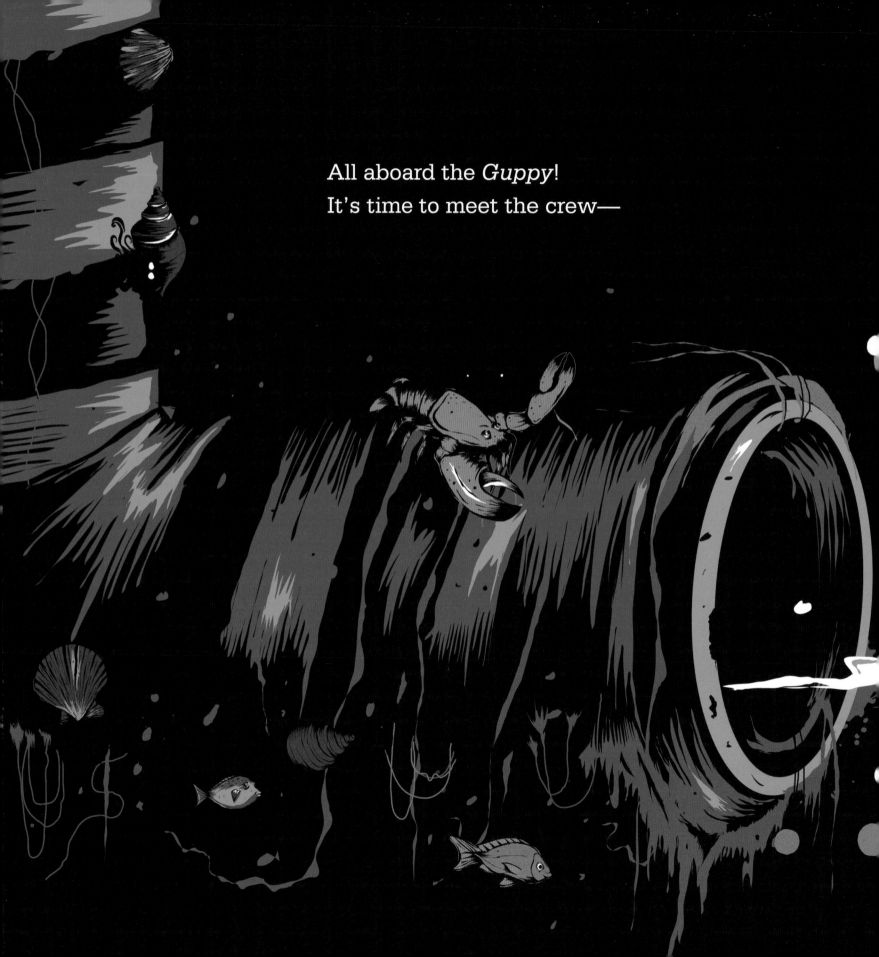

All aboard the *Guppy*!
It's time to meet the crew—

Deep-Sea Diver pilots the sub,
with Robot and Monkey, too!

Passing by a circus troupe,
they scout around for clues.

Their headlights track
a glowing trail—
a lead they must pursue.

Caught in a smack of jellyfish
afloat among the murk,
the gooey trail meanders through
this labyrinth of dessert.

While exploring the darkest corners
of a gloomy, ghostly wreck,
a cast of scuttling spider crabs
flee from a hungry threat.

Delving deep inside the wreckage,
through barnacle-battered pipes,
something bumps the *Guppy*'s rear,
and out go all the lights!

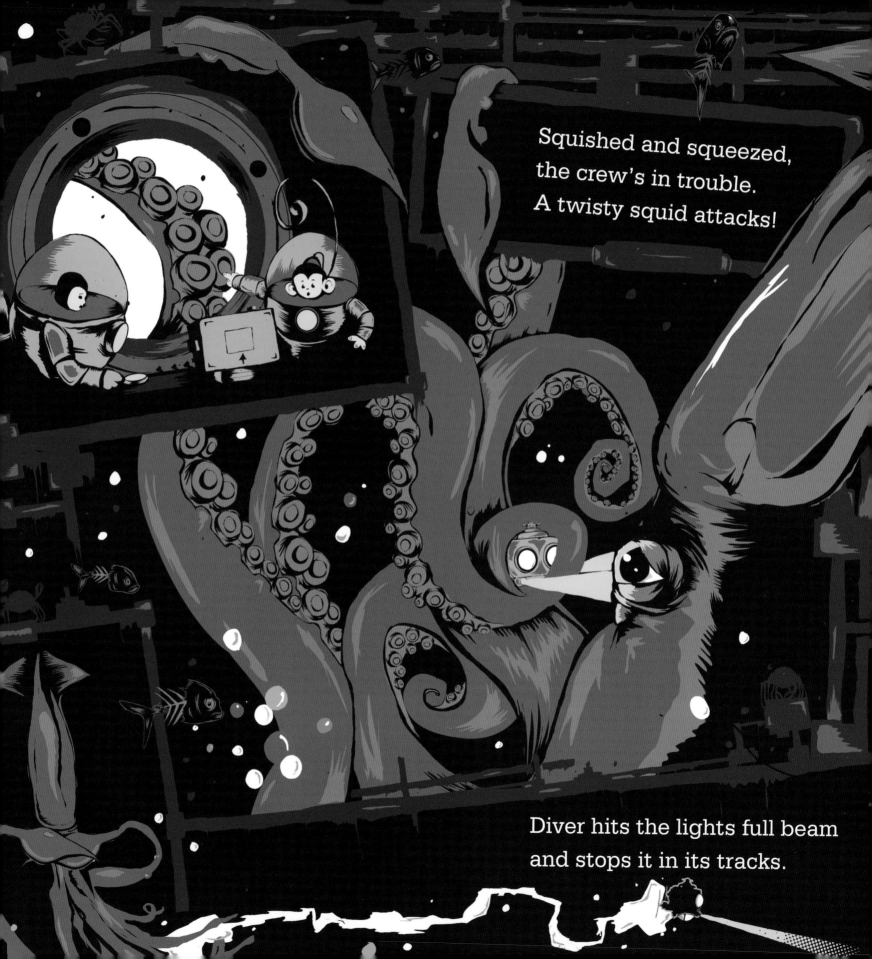

Squished and squeezed,
the crew's in trouble.
A twisty squid attacks!

Diver hits the lights full beam
and stops it in its tracks.

Bashed and bruised, the engine fails.
The *Guppy* needs repairs.
Robot wields his deep-sea tools,
fixing dents and tears.

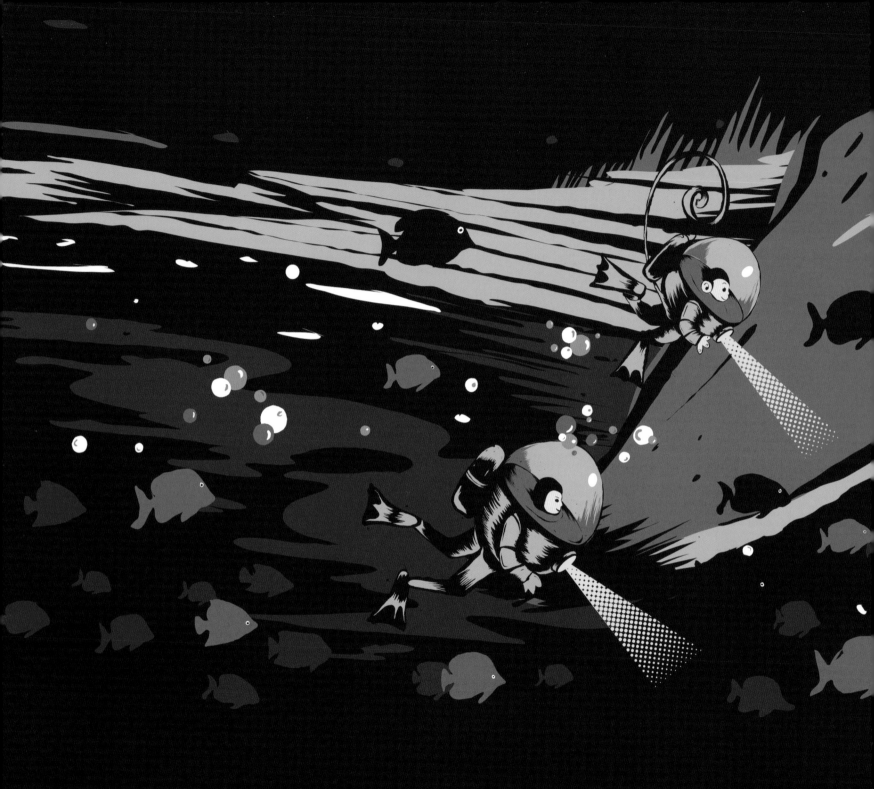

Diver and Monkey persevere
in pursuit of the slimy trail.

They hitch a rather cheeky ride
and carpool with a whale!

Beyond the
ancient ruins

buried deep among
the weeds,

the slimy trail
comes to an end.

But where does it
all lead?

Peering down a cavern,
they spy a golden glow—

the answer to this mystery
lies swallowed down below.

So deeper still they venture down
toward the glimmering light—
they're greeted by a galaxy
of starfish shining bright.

Having found the missing stars,
they're stuck down here together.
Unless they find a way out now,
they'll be trapped in here forever.

The divers have a rescue plan—
it's time to get to work.
Releasing gas from their scuba tanks,
they create an almighty . . .

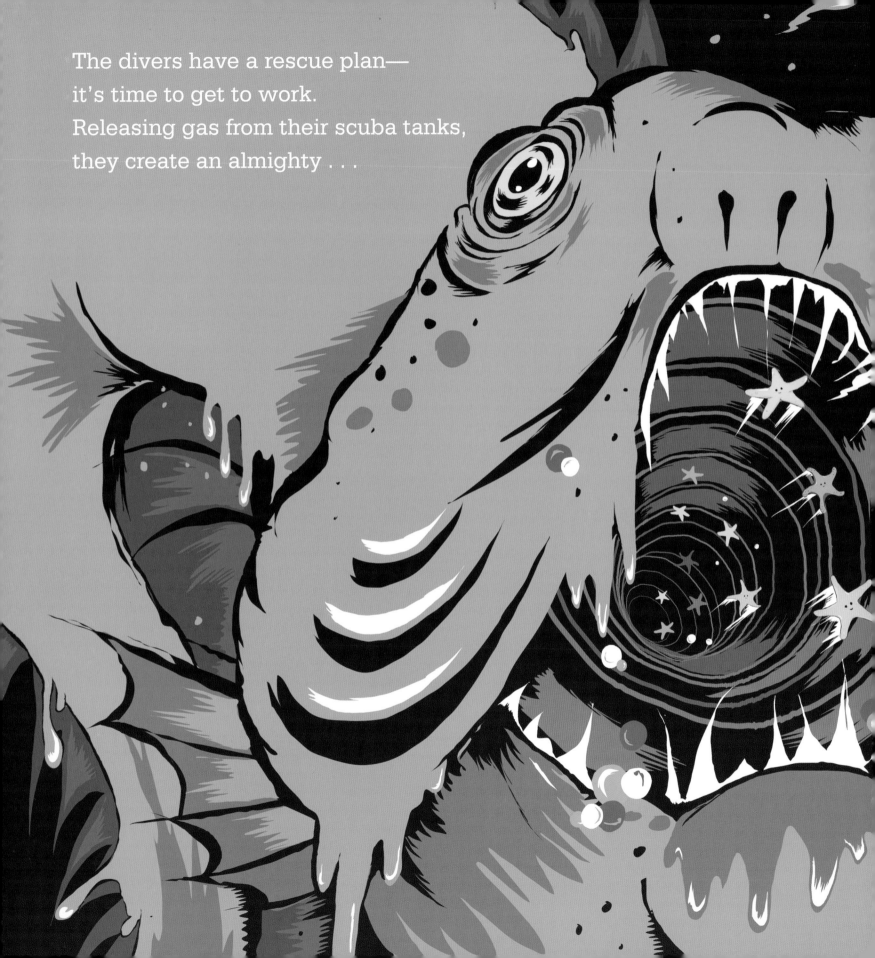

BURP!

Shooting out, the stars are saved!
The mystery's revealed.
The ocean's lights were swallowed up
by a slimy, belching eel!

Triumphant in their mission,
they've escaped the danger zone.
So for Diver, Monkey, and Robot,
it's time to go back home.

Beneath the secret lighthouse,
the lights have been restored—
the stars are beaming brightly
from the depths of the ocean floor.

The End